For Ruby, Ava, and Esme
S.W.

To my duckling, Luba, with endless love.
M.S.

First published in North America in 2013 by Boxer Books Limited.
First published in Great Britain in 2013 by Boxer Books Limited.
www.boxerbooks.com

The illustrations were prepared digitally by Manja Sojic
The text is set in Adobe Garamond Regular

ISBN 978-1-907967-46-7

1 3 5 7 9 10 8 6 4 2

Printed in Singapore

All of our papers are sourced from managed forests and renewable resources.

Are We There Yet?

Sam Williams   illustrated by Manja Stojic

Boxer Books

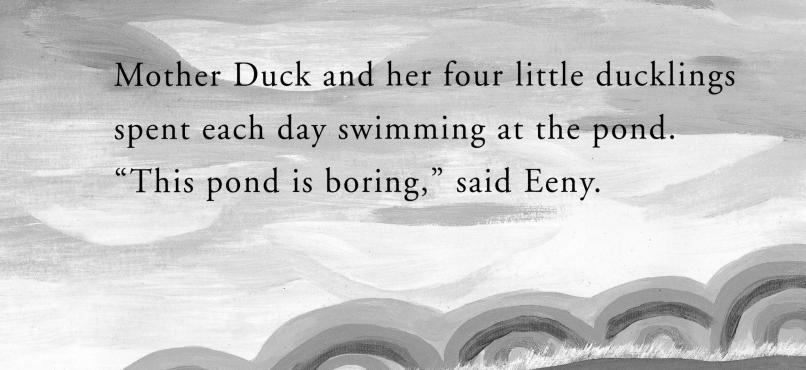

Mother Duck and her four little ducklings
spent each day swimming at the pond.
"This pond is boring," said Eeny.

"I'm tired of swimming," said Meeny.
"This pond is too small," said Miney.
"I love this pond," said Little Moe.

So Mother Duck decided to take
her ducklings on a trip.

They packed some duckweed sandwiches
and headed across the meadow.

Mother led her ducklings
through the buttercups.
Eeny followed her.
Meeny followed Eeny.
Miney followed Meeny.
And right at the end
came Little Moe.

After a while they passed
some ponies in a field.
"Look," said Mother, "ponies."
"They're boring," said Eeny.

"I bet they can't swim,"
said Meeny.
"Are we there yet?"
asked Miney.
"Neigh, neigh,"
said Little Moe.

And they waddled
on their way.

They saw some sheep on a hill.

"Look," said Mother, "sheep."

"They're woolly, and boring," said Eeny.

"I bet they can't swim," said Meeny.

"Are we there yet?" asked Miney.

"Baa, baa," said Little Moe.

And they waddled
on their way.

Soon they saw some cows.

"Look," said Mother, "cows."

"They're so slow, and boring," said Eeny.

"And they can't swim," said Meeny.

"Are we there yet?" asked Miney.

"Moo, moo," said Little Moe.

And they waddled on their way.

Next they saw some pigs.

"Look," said Mother, "pigs."

"They're so noisy, and boring,"
said Eeny.

"I'm sure they can't swim," said Meeny.

"Are we there yet?" asked Miney.

"Oink, oink," said Little Moe.

They waddled and they waddled.
"I'm tired and hungry," said Eeny.
"I want to go swimming,"
said Meeny.
"Are we there yet?" asked Miney.
"Duckweed sandwiches, please,"
said Little Moe.

So Mother stopped them for a rest,
and they had a picnic.

Then on and on they waddled.

"Are we there yet?" said Eeny.

"Are we there yet?" said Meeny.

"Are we there yet?" asked Miney.

"Quack, quack!" said Little Moe.

"Stop pushing me!" said Eeny.
"I did NOT push you!" said Meeny.

"Yes, you did. I saw you," said Miney.

"Now stop arguing," said Mother.

"Are we there yet?" asked Little Moe.

"I'm tired," said Eeny.

"So am I," said Meeny.

"Me too!" said Miney.

"Are we there yet?" asked Little Moe.

"Not far now,"
said Mother.

They came to a pond. "We're here!" said Mother.

"Our beautiful pond," said Eeny.

"I can go swimming," said Meeny.

"Our pond looks enormous!" said Miney.

"Hello, pond," said Little Moe.

And they quacked and splashed and swam until they couldn't swim any more.